LU & CLANCY

Sound Off

written by **Adrienne Mason**

illustrated by **Pat Cupples**

Kids Can Press

To Andrew — A.M.

To Judith, a truly great cat — P.C.

Text © 2002 Adrienne Mason
Illustrations © 2002 Pat Cupples

Kids Can Press acknowledges the financial support of the Ontario Arts Council,
the Canada Council for the Arts and the Government of Canada,
through the BPIDP, for our publishing activity.

Published in Canada by
Kids Can Press Ltd.
29 Birch Avenue
Toronto, ON M4V 1E2

Published in the U.S. by
Kids Can Press Ltd.
2250 Military Road
Tonawanda, NY 14150

www.kidscanpress.com

Edited by Valerie Wyatt and Stacey Roderick
Designed by Julia Naimska

Printed in Hong Kong, China, by Wing King Tong Company Limited

The hardcover edition of this book is smyth sewn casebound.
The paperback edition of this book is limp sewn with a drawn-on cover.

CM 02 0 9 8 7 6 5 4 3 2 1
CM PA 02 0 9 8 7 6 5 4 3 2 1

National Library of Canada Cataloguing in Publication Data

Mason, Adrienne
Sound off

(Lu & Clancy)
ISBN 1-55337-058-9 (bound).   ISBN 1-55337-059-7 (pbk.)

1. Sound — Juvenile literature. 2. Sound — Study and teaching —
Activity programs — Juvenile literature. I. Cupples, Patricia
II. Title. III. Series.

QC225.5.M38 2002   j534   C2001-904241-8

Kids Can Press is a *corus*™ Entertainment company

WHAT IS SOUND?

All of the activities in this book are about sound. Sound happens when air vibrates (moves very quickly). When you speak, or toot a horn, or bang a drum, you make the air vibrate. This moving air hits your eardrums and makes them vibrate, too. That is how you hear sound.

Chapter 1
Pest Control

"Quick, look up!"

Those were the last words Lu and Clancy heard before a water balloon flew through the window of their tree house. *Sploosh!* It burst, soaking them both.

"That's it," fumed Lu as she wiped the water out of her eyes. "Time to stop those pups."

Lu and Clancy, dog detectives, were babysitting Lu's sister, Sophie, and her friend Fanny. The two pups had pestered them all morning. First there had been the crank calls on the dog detectives' spy phone.

Then the treat of "special" lemonade made with soapy water. And now … water balloons!

"Those pups need something to keep them busy," said Clancy.

"What about building a house of cards?" asked Lu.

Clancy shook his head. "We need something that will tire them out."

"Climbing to the top of the apple tree?"

"Something that will *really* tire them out." Clancy paused, then he had an idea. "A hike to Mystic Lake and back should do the trick."

Chapter 2
Be Prepared

"Mystic Lake, here we come!" shrieked Sophie and Fanny.

Lu slung a small backpack over her shoulder. "I've got my gear," she said.

"Me, too," said Clancy. He smiled proudly at a mound of boots and buckets and sleeping bags.

"We aren't climbing Mount Everest," said Lu.

"You can never be too prepared." Clancy reached into the mound. "You might get caught in a snowdrift."

"Or see a rare bird in the bush."

"Or need to take a nap."

7

"Or need to solve a crime."

"We'll never get to Mystic Lake if we have to lug all this stuff," groaned Sophie and Fanny. But Clancy wouldn't leave anything behind. He stuffed his backpack until it bulged. When he ran out of room inside the pack, he tied things to the outside.

"Right," he said, heaving his pack onto his back. "March one, two, three, four. We're off to Mystic Lake!"

Chapter 3
Whistling Wanderers

"I'm hot," whined Sophie, wiping the sweat off her forehead.

"I'm thirsty," said Fanny, reaching for a water bottle.

Lu rolled her eyes. The pups were tired and complaining already!

Clancy finally caught up to them. Sweat was dripping off his nose. His tongue was hanging out. He was puffing so hard he could hardly speak.

"I'll check the map," he said weakly. He dived into his pack. The others relaxed in the shade of a big tree.

Ten minutes later, Clancy was still searching. Sophie and Fanny were getting bored. To keep them busy, Lu grabbed some drinking straws and scissors. She snipped here and there. Sophie and Fanny peered over her shoulder.

"Ta da!" Lu handed Sophie and Fanny the flutes she had made.

Before long, Sophie, Fanny and Lu were playing their flutes as they marched up the trail.

Tooty Flootey

Lu made flutes out of drinking straws. Here's how to make one.

You'll need:

- 2 large drinking straws
- scissors
- sticky tape

1. Cut the straws into 4 pieces of different lengths.

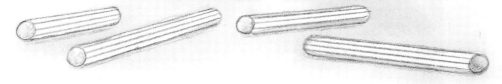

2. Lay the straws on the table. Line up one end of the straws.

3. Tape the straws together.

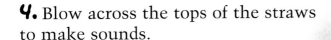

4. Blow across the tops of the straws to make sounds.

How it works

Different lengths of straws make different sounds. Why? Because there are different amounts of air inside each straw. The more air there is, the slower it vibrates, and the deeper the sound.

CHAPTER 4

BUZZ OFF

Clancy's head pounded. If I hear "Row, Row, Row Your Boat" one more time, I'll scream, he thought.

But before he had a chance to scream, he tripped over a root and went *splat!*

"Are you all right, Clancy?" asked Lu.

Clancy picked himself up. He brushed the dirt off his nose and nodded. "Let's eat. It looks like I've already unpacked lunch." He picked up the apples and sandwiches that had fallen out of his pack.

Lu spread out the picnic blanket. Clancy set out the food. Before long, all that was left were a few crumbs.

Lunch had made them sleepy. Clancy burped, then his eyelids drooped. Sophie and Fanny leaned back and yawned. Within minutes, they were fast asleep.

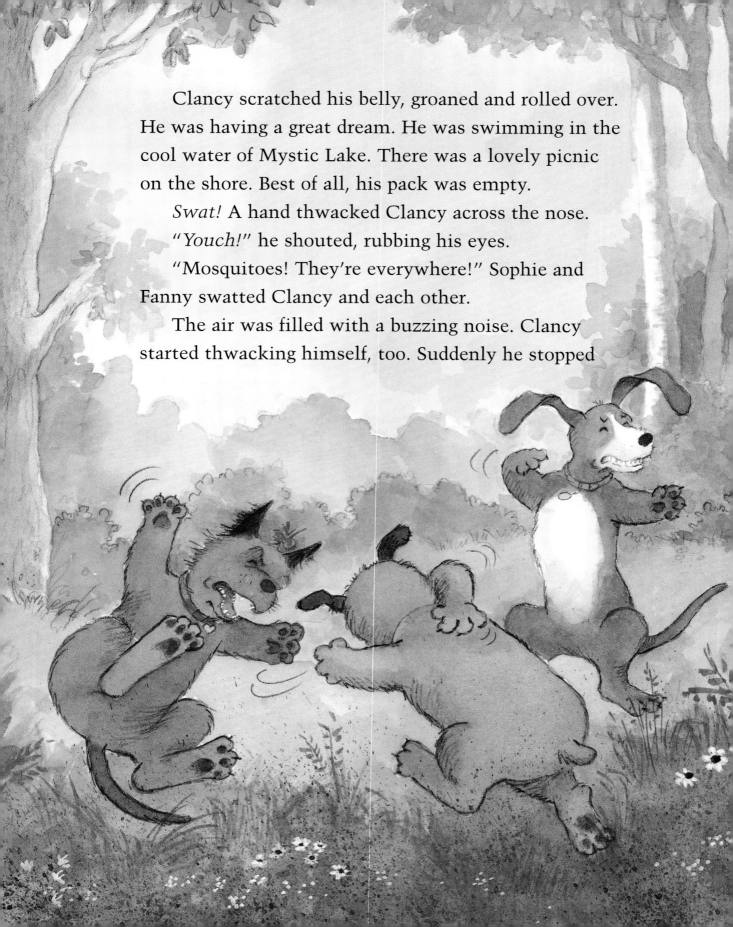

Clancy scratched his belly, groaned and rolled over. He was having a great dream. He was swimming in the cool water of Mystic Lake. There was a lovely picnic on the shore. Best of all, his pack was empty.

Swat! A hand thwacked Clancy across the nose.

"*Youch!*" he shouted, rubbing his eyes.

"Mosquitoes! They're everywhere!" Sophie and Fanny swatted Clancy and each other.

The air was filled with a buzzing noise. Clancy started thwacking himself, too. Suddenly he stopped

and looked around. "Wait a minute! There are no mosquitoes."

Sophie and Fanny stopped waving their arms. Clancy was right. There was buzzing, but no bugs.

Then they heard a snicker coming from behind a bush. Lu jumped out with a paper cup in her hand.

"Fooled you," she yelled. "My bug buzzer sure woke you up and got you moving. I caught a few mosquitoes and made them sound like a swarm. Now let's go. I can't wait for a swim!"

Bug Buzzer

To make a bug buzzer like Lu's, try this:

You'll need:

- a live insect (such as a fly)
- a paper cup
- a piece of waxed paper about 13 cm x 13 cm (5 in. x 5 in.)
- a rubber band

Note: Don't use stinging insects such as bees or wasps in this activity. When you're finished, release the insect.

1. Carefully capture the insect in the cup.

2. Place the waxed paper over the opening of the cup.

3. Wrap the waxed paper over the lip of the cup. Keep it in place with the rubber band.

4. Hold the bug buzzer to your ear and listen.

How it works

The vibrations from an insect's beating wings usually spread out in all directions, but the bug buzzer traps the vibrations. The vibrations make the waxed paper and the sides of the cup vibrate. This makes the sound louder.

Chapter 5
A Stormy Swim

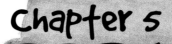
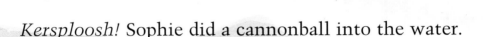

Kersploosh! Sophie did a cannonball into the water.

"Look out below!" Clancy did a belly flop.

They had finally arrived at Mystic Lake. And now they were *in* Mystic Lake.

The pups splashed and played. Soon they forgot the long, hard hike.

They also forgot to watch the weather.

Lu's eyes got as big as saucers. "Look!" She pointed to the sky.

A huge black cloud loomed over the hills. Streaks of lightning flashed to the ground. Thunder rumbled.

"Time to get out of here," yelled Clancy.

The pups dashed out of the water and behind some
bushes to change.

All of a sudden there was another yell. Only this
time it was more like a scream.

"Sophie!" shrieked Lu, running toward the bushes.
But all they found was Sophie's bikini. Sophie was gone!

Lu and Clancy looked at one another and gulped.
Fanny started to cry. Dark clouds were getting closer.
Sophie was missing. It was time for Lu and Clancy,
dog detectives, to spring into action.

"I'll get our detective kit while you search for clues," said Clancy. He pulled out a magnifying glass, fingerprint kit and camera. Then he started snapping pictures of the scene. Clancy was just about to take a picture of a small footprint when the sky got even darker. Rain began to pour down.

"The storm is moving in fast," Lu shouted above the thunder. "There's a cave behind those trees — let's hide there."

By the time they got to the cave, the storm was raging. Wind whipped the trees around. Lightning lit up the sky. Puddles were becoming ponds.

Fanny screamed as the thunder boomed. Even Clancy looked worried.

"Stay calm, Fanny," said Lu. "I think the storm is moving away."

"Hhhhhow do you know?" asked the trembling Fanny.

"Easy." Lu pointed to her watch. "I use this. I count the seconds between the lightning and the thunder. That tells me how far away the storm is."

Clancy and Fanny huddled around Lu's watch. The next time the lightning flashed, they started counting. "One, two, three …"

Storm Watching

Lu counted the seconds between the lightning
and the thunder to figure out how far away the storm was.
You can do it, too.

1. Start counting the seconds when you see lightning. Stop when you hear thunder.

2. Divide the number of seconds you counted by 3. This will tell you how many kilometers away the storm is. (Divide by 5 to find the distance in miles.)

3. Do the same thing every few minutes to see if the storm is coming closer or moving away.

How it Works

Light and sound travel in vibrating waves through the air. But light travels faster than sound. So by counting the seconds between when you see light (lightning) and hear sound (thunder), you can get a rough idea of how far away a storm is.

Chapter 6
Stormy Sounds

Lu was right! The storm was moving away. Before long the thunder rumbled far off in the distance. But the rain *was* still falling.

They took turns calling for Sophie.

Then Clancy had an idea. He buried his head in his backpack and started flinging things out. Soon he was dressed in rain gear from head to foot. He even had an umbrella. (Just in case.)

"I'm going out to search for Sophie," he announced. But he had only taken a few steps out of the cave when they heard the loudest, strangest sound.

"Yikes," said Clancy as he scampered back into the cave with his tail between his legs. "What was that?"

"It sounded like a mad moose," said Lu.

"Are there any monsters in these woods?" asked Fanny.

Chapter 7
A Fishing Trip

"Nobody panic," said Lu. She held Clancy's umbrella like a sword and stepped slowly out of the cave.

The noise started again. Lu jumped back into the cave. The noise stopped. She stepped out and back several times. Each time she went out, the noise started. When she went back in, the noise stopped.

"It must be watching us," said Fanny, her eyes wide. "What if it comes into the cave?"

But Lu wasn't listening. She stood quietly at the cave entrance. A smile came over her face. "Hey,

Clancy. Do you have a net in that pack?"

"Sure, but is this really the time to go fishing?"

"Any time is a good time to fish for little monsters," said Lu.

Lu and Clancy crept out of the cave and toward the sound. At first it sounded like a grunting moose. As they got closer, the grunting was followed by a snickering Sophie sound.

"Gotcha," they cried, as they trapped Sophie in the fishnet.

Moose Music

You can make a moose call just like Sophie did.

You'll need:

- a hammer
- a nail
- an empty tin can (a large coffee can is best)
- a piece of string

1. Ask an adult to hammer the nail into the bottom of the can.

2. Make a large knot in one end of the string. Feed the string through the hole in the can so that the knot is inside the can.

3. Dampen the string with some water. Hold the can under your arm. Pinch the string where it is closest to the can. Pull your fingers along the string to make a noise.

How it works

When you pull your fingers along the string, it vibrates. The can collects the vibrations and makes them sound louder. Thicker strings make a deeper sound because they vibrate more slowly than thinner strings. Experiment with different thicknesses of string or sizes of cans.

Chapter 8
Stormin' Mad

By the time Lu and Clancy had untangled Sophie from the net, it was getting dark. It was still raining, but not as hard as before. The wind and lightning had stopped. The storm was almost over.

"Time to head home," said Lu.

"But which way is home?" asked Fanny.

Lu and Clancy pointed in opposite directions.

It was raining. It was dark. And now they were lost.

"Looks like we'll have to stay here for the night," said Clancy.

"I'm cold," said Fanny.

"I'm hungry," said Sophie.

They hugged each other and started to whimper.

Clancy reached into his pack. "No problem — I came prepared." He pulled out blankets and candles and playing cards. Then he hauled out a huge chunk of chocolate. Next came a stove and a can of soup. Each time he reached into his pack, he pulled out another treat.

Before long Clancy's pack was empty, and they had a warm, cozy camp set up in the cave. They played card game after card game until Fanny fell asleep on Lu's shoulder.

"We've got a long day tomorrow," said Lu. "Time to join Fanny in lullaby land."

Sophie blew out the candle, and they snuggled under the blankets.

Just as Lu was drifting off to sleep, she heard the rain starting to pound down. Was that thunder, too? She shook Clancy.

"The storm is getting worse."

"Oh no!" said Clancy. "I can even hear the waves pounding on the shore. The storm must be right on top of us."

Lu lit the candle. In the sputtering light, they could see that the storm *was* right on top of them. Sophie was up to her tricks again. She was making the sounds of rain, crashing waves and thunder.

"Arrgh! Sometimes you make me so stormin' mad," groaned Lu. She rolled over and pulled the blanket over her head.

Storm Sounds

You can make the sounds of rain, waves and thunder.

You'll need:

- a large sheet of waxed paper
- sticky tape
- a saltshaker filled with salt
- a handful of dried peas
- a large plastic bowl
- a thin, flexible cookie sheet

To make rain, make a large cone out of waxed paper and tape it together. Hold the cone at an angle. Shake the salt so that it runs down the sides of the cone.

To make waves, put the peas in the bowl. Slowly tilt the bowl back and forth. The peas will slide along the bottom of the bowl and sound like waves.

To make thunder, hold the cookie sheet by one corner and shake it.

How it works

The cone shape of the rain-maker captures the sound of the salt moving and makes the sound louder. This is called an amplifier. The round bowl used to make the wave sound also acts as an amplifier. It makes the sound of the moving peas louder. Shaking the cookie sheet makes big, fast vibrations in the air that sound like thunder.

Chapter 9
Sound to the Rescue

Lu woke up and rubbed her eyes. All she heard was snoring dogs. They'd made it through the night safe and sound.

She shook Clancy awake. "We have to make noise so someone will find us."

"How about this noise?" mumbled Clancy. He rolled over and started snoring again.

Lu went to the entrance of the cave and gave a loud yodel. "Yo do lay de hoo!" Clancy, Fanny and Sophie sat bolt upright. Soon Lu had them perched on top of the cave calling for help.

They took turns singing, yelling and yodeling until they were hoarse. Still no rescuers arrived.

"We need to make a noisier noise," said Lu. "Any bells or horns in your pack, Clancy?"

"Nope, but what about this stuff?" Clancy pointed to a pile of garbage left over from the night before.

"What good is that junk?" asked Sophie.

Clancy picked up some of the garbage and started snipping and twisting and taping it together.

"To the untrained eye, it looks like garbage. But I see drums, guitars and kazoos." In a few minutes, he passed out the instruments he had made.

Before long, a wild sound was coming from the cave. Lu, Clancy, Sophie and Fanny banged, strummed and tooted their hearts out. They were still playing away two hours later when their rescuers arrived.

The Junk Band

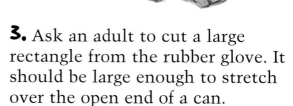

Sophie's tin drum

You'll need:

- a can opener
- 3 empty cans of the same size
- duct tape or electrical tape
- scissors
- an old rubber glove
- a rubber band

1. With an adult's help, use the can opener to remove the bottoms from all 3 cans.

2. Place one can on the ground. Put a second can on top of it. Tape them together. Tape the third can to the top of the second can.

3. Ask an adult to cut a large rectangle from the rubber glove. It should be large enough to stretch over the open end of a can.

4. Stretch the piece of rubber glove over the opening of the top can. Secure it with a rubber band.

5. Hold the drum between your knees and bang on the rubber top.

Clancy's guitar

You'll need:

- a shoebox without a lid
- 3–4 rubber bands of different lengths and thicknesses

1. Stretch the rubber bands around the box.

2. Pluck the rubber bands to play the guitar.

Fanny's cardboard kazoo

You'll need:

- a hole punch
- a cardboard tube from a toilet paper roll
- a 10 cm x 10 cm (4 in. x 4 in.) piece of waxed paper
- a rubber band

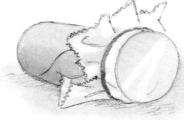

1. Use the hole punch to make a hole halfway down the cardboard tube.

2. Place the waxed paper over one end of the tube. Hold it in place with the rubber band.

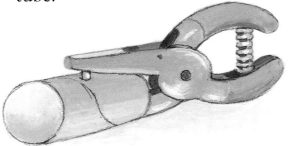

3. Hum into the open end of the tube.

Lu's loud screamer

You'll need:

- 10 cm x 10 cm (4 in. x 4 in.) piece of waxed paper or cellophane

1. Stretch the waxed paper tightly between your hands, and hold it in front of your lips as shown.

2. Purse your lips, and blow hard and fast on the edge of the waxed paper.

How it works

The drum: When you bang the drum, you make the rubber vibrate. Its vibrations make the air vibrate, which you hear as sound.

The guitar: When you pluck a rubber band, it starts to vibrate. Thin rubber bands and ones that are tightly stretched make a high sound because they vibrate quickly. Thick rubber bands and ones that are loosely stretched make a low sound because they vibrate more slowly.

The kazoo: Humming makes the air vibrate. When you hum into the kazoo, the vibrations are trapped. They make the cardboard tube and waxed paper vibrate, too. This makes the sound of your humming louder.

The loud screamer: The air you blow moves very quickly, which makes the thin waxed paper vibrate quickly. The faster the air and waxed paper vibrate, the higher the sound.

Chapter 10
Safe and Sound

Clancy picked up a nightgown and examined it with his magnifying glass. Lu was studying fingerprints on a clothespin.

They were finally back in their tree house and could get back to work. Carlotta, a collie down the road, was missing some laundry. Lu and Clancy were helping solve the crime.

Sophie and Fanny were sitting on the tree house roof. They were still tooting and banging away on the instruments they'd made. They were loud and off key, but that didn't stop them. They played day and night. They were even planning to give lessons to the kids in the neighborhood.

Lu and Clancy didn't seem to notice the racket. They just smiled at each other and adjusted their earmuffs.

"Aah," said Clancy. "Now that is music to my ears."